THEY TWINKLED
LIKE JEWELS

Start Publishing PD LLC
Copyright © 2024 by Start Publishing PD LLC

Start Publishing PD is a registered trademark of Start Publishing PD LLC
Manufactured in the United States of America

Cover art: Shutterstock/Taisiya Kozorez

Cover design: Jennifer Do

10 9 8 7 6 5 4 3 2 1

ISBN 979-8-8809-2321-2

1

The thing can be traced back, now, to its beginning. Back to a certain night in April, to the auditorium of the Boston Science institute, where Dr. Walton delivered his epochal lecture.

A lecture that few enough heard, at the time. Nor is that wonderful. Outside the night was warm and luring, the first breath of spring for a winter-weary world. It is hardly strange that the audience that night was a small one.

Yet when Walton emerged onto the stage with the Institute's president, he did not seem to notice the rows of empty seats. He was a quick, nervous little man of middle age, with thick, black hair through which he constantly ran his right hand, and black eyes that flashed restlessly about. While the smiling rotund president introduced him to the audience, with a few bland and cheerful inanities, Walton was fidgeting nervously in his seat, and when the other had stepped back, with a concluding eulogistical phrase, the little scientist sprang at once to the front of the stage, being greeted by a ripple of mild applause. At once he started to speak, with staccato rapidity.

"The title of my lecture," he began, "'*Evolution and the Future*,' is somewhat ambiguous, so I will say now that it is not my intention to discuss old theories, but to present a new one. Yet for my purpose, it is necessary to bring to your attention first the general theory of evolution, as it is now known.

"As you know, before the promulgation of that theory, it was generally believed that all species, all races of living creatures, had always possessed the same form and nature, and always would. It was not thought possible that in time a creature or race of creatures could change entirely in nature and bodily form, develop, that is, into a higher state of existence.

"Then came the great work of Darwin and Wallace and Huxley. It became clear that the only constant thing in our world is change, that instead of remaining always in the same forms, life constantly changes and develops into new forms. Up from the first plasmic slime, the base of all life on earth, life has advanced through a thousand different forms, up a thousand branching paths. Sea-slime—jellyfish—invertebrates—reptiles—mammals—man —up, up, always up, striving, climbing, every generation a tiny bit ahead of the previous generation, a tiny bit farther advanced along the road of evolution. We know not where that road leads, for our path of evolution, like the paths all life must follow, was laid down for us, as I believe, by a Power above earth. So, although we know not what forms we are changing into, or what forms all other living things change into, we do know that that change is going on, infinitely slowly, but steadily. How much higher the human race today than the savage Neanderthal men of fifty thousand years ago! And fifty thousand years from now, men will be as much above us. It is the same with all life, with all forms of life. All go up, up, change and change.

"We cannot swerve aside from the path of change we follow. But suppose we could speed up our progress, could travel faster up that path? Suppose we were able to accelerate the process of evolution so that a thousand years of evolutionary development could be crowded into a single day?

"Such a suggestion sounds mad, almost. Evolution is the slowest process of nature, and how could it be accelerated? To discover that, we must discover the cause of evolution itself, must find out why we change, why all life changes.

"That question, the cause of evolution, is the great riddle of biology. Countless explanatory theories have been advanced, adaptations, segregation, mutations, Mendelism—I could recount a dozen such, but all such explanations have failed, and the cause of the evolutionary change has remained a mystery. A mystery which I have finally solved. And the answer, the force that drives life up its myriad roads of change, the very cause of evolution itself, is—the Garner ray.

"I imagine that the name is unfamiliar to most of you. It is only within the last few years that the Garner ray has been isolated, by the physicist whose name it bears. Even yet, the nature of the ray has remained largely a mystery. We know, however, that the earth, the universe, is one vast welter of vibrations, visible and invisible. From this ruck of vibratory forces we can pick a few that are known to science. The Hertzian rays—that is, the radio waves—and chemical rays, heat rays, light rays, a vast welter, I repeat, of vibratory forces.

"And the Garner ray is one of these. It is thought to be a new kind of chemical ray, having its source in vast masses of radioactive substances in the earth's interior. It is also thought that the ray is altered, somehow, by the magnetic currents that race between the poles. Whatever its origin, it is known that in some places on the earth the ray seems exceptionally strong, while in other spots it is rather weak. This is taken to mean that the radioactive materials that are its source are unevenly distributed in the earth's interior.

"You will want to know what connection this ray has with the subject of evolution. It has such a connection, and I have been the first to find it. We know the profound effects that the other vibratory forces have on life. Light rays, for instance: how changed life would be without them! And this Garner ray has an equally important effect on life, for it is the constant action of this ray, affecting the nerve centers in a way I cannot explain, that changes all of us, mentally and physically, that changes all life, that causes the evolution change itself. Since the first presence of life on earth, the action of this ray has driven it upward to its present levels, and still drives it upward, slowly, but unceasingly.

"And I have proof that this is so. Physicists have found that in the continent of Australia the ray is weakest on earth, due, no doubt, to the fact that the radio-active bases of it are scarce in the earth beneath the island continent. The ray is weakest there, has always been weakest there, and what is the result? Any zoologist will tell you that Australia abounds with strange animals found no place else on earth, that evolution there seems retarded, slower, It is so even with human beings there. The native Australian, the bushman, is without doubt the lowest form of human being on earth, the least developed of all the races of men.

"I come now to the heart of my interest. I have shown you that this Garner ray, acting on all life on earth, has caused all the evolutionary changes of the past. I have shown you that where the ray is strongest the course of evolution is most rapid, and vice versa. Now suppose that we were able to produce this ray artificially, as we produce light and heat and radio waves artificially. Suppose we produced this Garner ray in the laboratory, then concentrated it, condensed it, focused it, and turned it on a human being. What would be the result?"

Walton paused and held up a lean finger to emphasize his words. "When that is done, when an artificial Garner ray is produced and turned onto a human body, the possessor of that body will be thrown thousands of years ahead in mental and physical development, will be thrown ages ahead of the rest of us in point of evolutionary standing.

"And if the same thing were done to all of us it would have the same effect on all, would take us ahead thousands, millions of years in development, depending on the strength of the artificial ray. Think of the countless ages it took life to crawl up to the present human form. And then, after those eons of painful progress, this mighty jump, this great short-cut. Seven-league boots for humanity, on the road of evolution!

"And this is no vain dream. It will be accomplished. I do not say that I can accomplish it myself, but it will be done, if not in our time, in some time to come. It will be done, and then—the great transformation. I seem to see humanity leaping up to full stature at once, springing from achievement to achievement, strong and conquering. I seem to see men become like gods—"

2

Even now one remembers the uproar created by Walton's astounding statements. An uproar that spread over the scientific world, and into the newspapers, making a world-figure of the obscure Boston scientist. And, too, making him one of the most denounced men in the world.

For his theories found no shadow of acceptance. Nine scientists out of ten, when asked for opinions, had it that Walton was either deluding himself, or was an outright charlatan. Evolution, they pointed out, was, after all, only a theory. A great theory, a basically important theory, but still a theory. It belonged more to philosophy than to science. So when Walton treated evolution as a laboratory matter, and calmly proposed to speed up the process, it seemed plain to them that he was either slightly crazy or a skillful publicity-seeker.

Thus Walton found himself universally condemned, and strangely enough, seemed to mind it not at all. Luckily for him, he was not dependent on an academic position for his existence, since he had an ample inherited income. So, quite unaffected by the storm he had raised, he went calmly on with his work, spending most of his time in the little laboratory building behind his home.

This home of his was an inherited, old-fashioned mansion, a big, rambling house that had formerly stood at the center of an estate, but was not surrounded by the neat bungalows of a modem suburb. Behind it stood the little brick building that held his laboratory, and although Walton had made no statements after his lecture, he was generally believed to be at work testing his theories in that place. None could say for certain, though, for Walton had but few friends and admitted only one of these into the laboratory.

The single favored one was Stuart Owen, a young physician who had just returned after a month's absence from the city, and who was eager to learn more of the turmoil Walton had stirred up. So, directly after his return, he had hurried out to his friend's home to hear more about the matter.

As the two friends entered the main room of the laboratory building, a man working at a table there rose and came to meet them. This was Brilling, Walton's assistant, a silent, hawk-nosed and thin-lipped young man who mumbled a few words of greeting and then hurried back to his work. Owen then seized the opportunity to satisfy the question in his mind.

"This evolution business, Walton," he began; "you were hardly serious about that, were you? I read the reports of your lecture in the papers. You aren't really working on a thing like that, are you?"

"No, I was quite in earnest," Walton assured him. "Brilling and I have been working on the thing for nearly two years."

Owen's face showed his surprise. "But man," he protested, "it sounds silly, almost. To speed up evolution—you'll never succeed."

Walton smiled slightly, and exchanged a significant glance with his assistant. Then: "But I have succeeded," he said, quietly.

As Owen looked his amazement, he went on, "I suppose I can trust you to keep the matter a secret for the present,

Owen?" And at the other's swift nod, he continued, "Well, look over here," leading the way to a long work-bench.

A litter of electrical apparatus covered the bench's surface, and in a clear space to one side stood a small cylindrical case of black insulating material, which was studded on its top with a number of small nickel switches and connected by a dozen wires to the electrical instruments on the bench. Laying a hand on the case, Walton remarked, "The fruit of a year's work. This little instrument, Owen, is capable of producing an artificial Garner ray that is many times stronger than the natural ray. It is powerful enough to affect anything inside this room, to throw anything living in the room ages ahead in evolutionary development. The ray itself is a chemical ray, produced by a combination of radio-active elements inside the case, but it is changed and altered by a series of small but powerful electro-magnets through which it passes."

As Owen regarded the black cylinder dubiously, Walton said, "I see that I'll have to convince you another way," and made a gesture to Brilling, who left the room, returning in a few minutes with a live chicken.

Placing the chicken on the floor beneath the bench, Walton took from a drawer three narrow pads of gray cloth, one of which he handed to Owen, and another to Brilling. As Owen examined the thing, perplexed by its unlooked-for weight, Walton told him, "A shield for you, Owen, to protect you from the ray. When this is strapped around your body, covering your spine, the ray will have no effect on you. It can't penetrate through the lining of metal foil in these pads, and thus the vital spinal nerve-centers are protected."

When Owen had awkwardly adjusted the shield to Walton's satisfaction, his friend exclaimed, "Now watch," and reaching over to the black case, snapped on a tiny switch, then stepped back and pointed toward the chicken on the floor.

Owen looked, then gasped with astonishment. For the chicken was changing— changing. As he watched, the wings became smaller and smaller, shriveled away and vanished, the feathers became sparse and disappeared also, the fowl became ever more small, dwindled, contracted until it was hardly larger than a robin, then fell dead, a shrunken little bundle of skin and bone. Owen looked up, to meet Walton's smiling eyes.

"You see?" asked Walton, snapping off the switch. "You have just seen the entire future of a species, have seen, in a few minutes, the changes that species will go through in the next few ages.

He turned to Brilling, who again left the room, returning with another chicken.

"I'm going to reverse the process now," Walton said, "and throw this one back in development. In other words, you say the future of the species, now I'll show you the past."

"But how—?" Owen began, then his words were broken into by Walton's swift explanation.

"Easy enough. Once I had found out how to produce the Garner ray, the ray that accelerates evolution, I looked for a ray that would do the exact opposite, that would reverse evolution. And I found that all that was necessary to produce a reversing ray was to reverse the current in the electromagnets that alter the ray. So this reversing ray is the exact opposite of the Garner ray, the accelerating ray, and has an exactly opposite effect. Therefore, unless you want to be thrown back a million years in development, see that your spine-shield is on all right." And he laughed as Owen nervously adjusted the pad.

Walton placed the second fowl in the same position as the first, but took time first to secure it to the floor by two large steel shackles which he attached to its legs, and which were chained to the floor. At Owen's questioning glance he smiled. "A necessary precaution," he said; then, reaching toward the ray-producing case, snapped on another switch, stepping instantly aside when he had done so.

As Owen watched the creature on the floor, fascinated, it changed as swiftly as the first, but grew in size instead of dwindling, seemed to pass with lightning speed through a hundred different forms, changing into a large-sized, fierce-looking bird with coarse, heavy plumage and a long feathered tail, with jaws instead of a beak, jaws that were lined with sharp teeth.

"Archaeopteryx," said Walton, and Owen started. An archaeopteryx, the first known bird, creature of the Reptilian Age! Even as he stared at the thing it was changing again, passing into a true reptile form, a leathery-skinned thing that strained at the shackles holding it. Then there was a swift flashing through a myriad half-glimpsed reptilian forms, passing down through a chain of slimy sea-creatures; and suddenly the change had stopped, and on the floor lay a little heap of slimy, viscous substance.

"Protoplasmic sea-slime," said Walton; "the first and lowest base of life."

Owen found that his hands were trembling. As Walton

snapped off the switch on the case, he called to him, "Good God, Walton, can you do that with any creature?" And he pointed a tremulous finger at the slimy mass on the floor.

"I can," Walton told him, "and as soon as I have made experiments on a big scale with the accelerating ray, I'll try it on a human being—a willing subject, of course. I will try to throw him ahead enough to give him advanced mental and physical powers, without taking him too far."

"On a big scale," Owen repeated, "how can you do that? If you spread that accelerating ray over a big territory, who knows what people might be caught by its power, and changed? Who knows what would happen?"

Walton waved away the objection. "I've thought of that, Owen. And consequently, we're going to work out the thing where it will be absolutely safe to do so, that is, on an island. A little island town in the West Indies, a few hundred miles south of Cuba, which I bought at a ridiculously low price. It's entirely uninhabited, now. So that's my plan. To set up a larger ray-projector that will cover the whole island with its power, then get a lot of different animals and turn them loose there. You see the idea? Every living thing on the island will be under the influence of the accelerating ray, and thus everything on the island will be thrown ahead in evolutionary development. We can see hundreds of thousands of years of development, condensed into a few weeks or months. Of course Brilling and I will wear the shields, to protect ourselves, but everything else will change, and we can keep records of every change in each species, photographs and notes, and such. It's all planned out, Owen. Brilling and I sent our equipment down to a Cuban port some time ago, and we're leaving ourselves next week, for the island."

"I don't like it," Owen told him. "There's something ghastly about the whole idea. You know that I'm not a superstitious man, but this plan of yours—why, you're twisting the very basic laws of nature, Walton, and no one ever tried that yet but came to wreck."

Walton's face was dreaming, abstracted. "No, Owen, every achievement of science has been heralded as a tampering with nature. And this will be the greatest thing ever accomplished for humanity, if we can go through with it. If our experiments down there are successful we will try it on the human body. Think of it, Owen: thousands, millions of years of development, accomplished in a flash. If we can do it—"

Owen did not answer, and a silence fell over the three men. As he left the laboratory, he looked back and saw on the floor the shining heap of slime there. A vague, doubting fear ran through him, an oppressing foreboding of evil.

And that weighting fear clung again to him, a week later, as he watched a rusty tramp steamer go out from a New York dock, bearing with it Walton and Brilling, who had contracted to be put ashore at the Cuban port where their equipment awaited them. Owen watched the boat warp through the foggy mists of early morning, then walked slowly back from the dock's edge.

It was only then that it occurred to him that he had no way of communicating with Walton, short of going to the island itself. The outcome of the whole matter would remain in doubt for him until Walton came back. Until Walton came back! But

would he ever come back?

Would he?

3

Walton came back. He came back a year later, on a stormy night in May, when the wind was lashing the deserted streets with gusts of cold rain. Owen, lounging in his rooms over a dull novel, heard a sudden knocking at his door, and when he flung the door open, a wet and shabby figure staggered in, that he knew at once was his friend. During all that year he had had no word from Walton, and now, as he pulled out a chair for the dripping, swaying figure before him, he could restrain his questions no longer.

Slumped in the chair, staring fixedly at the opposite wall, Walton did not seem to hear his eager queries. Owen noticed then that the man seemed years older, his face drawn and haggard, his eyes dazed. But at a word in Owen's speech, sudden life leapt into his expression.

"The island," he repeated; "yes, I come from there, Owen."

"And Brilling?" asked Owen.

"He is—alive," was the slow answer.

Shocked by the utter change in his friend, Owen was silent. For minutes Walton stared vacantly ahead, then seemed to pull himself together, to become conscious of his surroundings, for the first time. Turning to Owen, he said slowly, as though repeating a lesson, "I must go back, Owen."

"You mean back to the island?" asked the other, and Walton nodded.

"I must go back," he repeated, "and soon. I came to you—I can tell you—" Again he fell silent, but Owen did not disturb him, waiting until he spoke again.

With an effort, Walton resumed the thread of his speech. "The island—we went there, Brilling and I. That was only a year ago, Owen. Only a year ago!" He seemed to muse on the thought.

"But Brilling and I went there, you remember. We went to Lluegos, a Cuban port, first, and arranged to have our equipment taken down to the island for us. We took native labor down, and got the place ready, building a cottage for living quarters, and a small laboratory, and setting up our equipment there, arranging our supplies. And we brought animals down to the island, and turned them loose there.

"We got most of the animals from the menagerie of a little traveling circus that had stranded in Lluegos. The hotel proprietor there was holding the menagerie of the show for an unpaid bill, and was glad enough to sell them for next to nothing. So we had them taken down to the island and turned loose there. There was a mangy old lion, a couple of splendid young leopards, wolves, and so on. Of course we had a stockade around the cottage and laboratory, to keep them from getting too close.

"When all that had been done, Brilling and I were the only men on the island, having got rid of the laborers we had hired, as soon as their work was done. We had a small boat, a yawl, to come and go in, and equipment. The main feature was a big ray-projector, like the one you saw, but much larger and more powerful, capable of throwing its ray over the whole extent of

the island. Of course, Brilling and I wore the shields night and day, for our own protection.

"All was ready, so we began, turning on the accelerating ray, though not using near the full power at our command. We wanted the change to be slow enough to record, you see. Two days went by and we could see no change, but on the third day we noticed a changing in the lion and the leopards. The three big cats were getting smaller, were dwindling in size every hour, it seemed. In five days they had become as small as house-cats, and were as tame. The seventh day, we found them dead.

"You see what it meant? We had seen, in seven days, the whole future development of those two feline species, had seen the fate of all their kind, in the future, and it was just what we had expected. Ever since the time of the saber-tooth tiger, the larger felines on earth have tended to become ever smaller and less ferocious. And thus we had seen the ultimate end of the species, a dwindling into mere cats.

"After that first transformation, the changes came thick and fast. The wolves changed next, changed in nature, becoming as tame and gentle as dogs. They became dogs, in fact. Then they began to grow, grew to a great size, became as large as horses, indeed, but for all their giant size, they stayed as tame as ever. Finally they dwindled too, and died away. It was the end of that species. And the changes still went on.

"We were living in a biologist's paradise, Owen, were seeing the whole future course of evolution, seeing the future development of a myriad different species. With rifles for our protection we ranged the island constantly, photographing and recording the changes we saw, constantly observing the beasts as they developed, watching, watching. We spared time only to eat and sleep.

"We kept the ray-projector always going, always sending out the accelerating ray, and always the things on the island changed. Not only the animals we had brought, but the things that had always lived on the island. Snakes, for instance. There were many of these, and under the accelerating ray they developed into horrible forms. Some grew to python size, and even larger, while some developed short legs and webbed feet, on which they walked and ran. And some took to the water, as their nature changed. But in time all died away, disappeared.

"After the snakes had died away, the birds on the island began to change. Most of these died soon, but one breed evolved that lasted for a few weeks, a great condor-like thing with brilliant plumage, a giant bird of prey that was the fiercest thing on the island. It attacked us whenever we ventured out, and we were glad when it died too.

"And still the changes went on. Still the ray forced the life on the island up and up in development. After the birds, there came a change in the insect life of the place, and a wave of strange monsters swept over the island. Gigantic spiderlike beasts, monstrous flying creatures that were like great wasps, in some ways, but were the size of airplanes, and proportionately fierce. All the insect life on the island seemed to be developing into new and monstrous forms, that made the place a hell to live in. Some of the things we only glimpsed. There was a worm-thing, for instance, vast and white and sluggish, a hundred feet in length, that flopped about in a swamp and uttered hoarse, bellowing cries. We heard it at night, sometimes. . . And there were others, even worse. But in time all the insect monsters died away, as the others had done before them.

"And, to replace them, came giant reptilian creatures from the sea, strange sea-monsters of some future age. You see, the ray acted on the waters around the island, too, and had the same accelerating effect on all the life in them. So it was that we glimpsed strange things in the sea around us, vast scaled and fanged creatures that fought and tore with inconceivable ferocity. They were beasts of some future age, but they seemed to us like the hideous dinosaurs of the past, so large and fierce were they. Some of them were amphibian, and they made life precarious for us by venturing onto the island and lumbering about, crashing through the forests and meeting and battling with each other.

*

"The island was a strange place, then. And even after the sea-monsters had passed, Owen, it was strange, a place of silence and death, for the ray had wiped out all animal life on the island, had thrown all life ahead and ahead in development until all had died away. There could be no more changes, we thought. And we were wrong, Owen. We were wrong.

"For there came another change, a last, great change, a terrible change that neither Brilling nor I had foreseen. And that was a change in the plant-life on the island, in the vegetation. All animal life on the place had changed and passed, and now the plant-life was changing.

"Yet we might have expected such a change. Evolution rules

all plant-life, just as it does all animal life. Just as all present species of animals have come up from the beasts of the Mesozoic Age, so have all present species of plants come up from the giant ferns and conifers of that age. All plant-life on earth is slowly developing, the same as animal life. And under the accelerating ray, that slow evolution of the plant-life on the island began to speed up, after all animal life there had passed.

"The plants changed, Owen. Trees, bushes, weeds, they shot up into strange new forms, dwindled and passed and rose to still other forms, and finally, after weeks of such changes, one type of plant began to become dominant on the island, to crowd out all the others. This was a plant much like a large cactus in appearance, but a plant that seemed almost animal in its activity and intelligence. It could wave its great feelers about, and exhibited many signs of its growing intelligence. And gradually its roots began to wither away, gradually it became able to move about at will, no longer tied to one spot by its roots.

"I understood what we were seeing. I understood then that sometime in the far future, when all animal life has died away from earth, the reign of the plants will begin, that a race of plants will evolve into the uppermost form of life, just as a race of animals, man, is the uppermost form now. I saw that long after man had gone down to extinction, the world would be ruled by intelligent active plants.

"And I became afraid, Owen. Who could say what degree of power these plant-things on the island might not attain, if left to grow unhindered? If we allowed them to go forward in development, under the accelerating ray, we might loose an evil, spawning horror upon the world, a thing that should not be, in our time.

"And, too, I felt that my reason was going, after all the things I had seen. I felt that I must get back to the world of men, that I must make some contact with my fellow-humans if I wanted to preserve a balanced mind. So I proposed to Brilling that we turn on the reversing ray, throwing the plant-things back to harmless vegetation, then leave the island and spend a month or so in one of the West Indian cities.

"Brilling refused. He felt none of my fears, was entirely absorbed in the things we were doing. He urged me to go, though, and finally I did so, taking the yawl and heading for Jamaica. Brilling said that he wanted to study the development of the plant-things a few days more, but promised to turn on the reversing ray within the next few days, and I was content with his promise. So I left, leaving Brilling on the island alone—except for the plant-things.

"I had my month in Kingston, Owen, and then my thoughts turned back to the island. It had been our plan to get a new lot of animals and turn them loose on the island like the first bunch, then turn on the reversing ray and watch their changes as they went back down through the evolutionary development of the past. I was eager to get started on this, so at the end of the month I left Kingston and went to the island. I went back, and I found—

"How can I describe what I found? I found all my former fears realized, and found new horror, too. I saw for the first time why Brilling had wanted to stay on the island.

"He had turned the accelerating ray on himself, Owen, had

removed the shield from his body and had allowed the ray to throw him forward ages in development. And I saw him, saw the shape that was his, the shape and form of all humanity, ages from now.

"His head had grown very much larger, Owen, had grown to almost twice its former size, and had become quite hairless, though the features seemed much the same. But the body! Owen, there was no body, as we know it! Instead of a human body, the head was attached directly to a mass of flesh, round and squat, which was about half the size of a human trunk. And from this shapeless mass projected four supple, boneless arms of muscles, arms that were really long, powerful *tentacles*. He could walk on these tentacles, or on part of them, or he could use all to grasp and hold. Four long twisting tentacles, that had once been arms and legs. For I saw in Brilling the changes that future ages will work in the human body. You know, Owen, that the human body tends constantly to become simpler, less complex in organization. The toes grow smaller, less prehensile and shrink away, the hair disappears, and certain organs of the body, like the appendix, become entirely useless, atrophied. All our complex digestive and respiratory apparatus tends always to become simpler. And I saw in Brilling, the cumulative effects of ages of such changes.

"And he had changed mentally, too. He knew me, his mind retained all its former memories and knowledge, but it had acquired also new thoughts, new ambitions, new desires. Struck with horror at the change in him, I proposed to turn the reversing ray on him and throw him back to a normal human body, but when I made that suggestion, he was furious. A body like mine, he declared, would be loathsome to him. It was just as if I had suggested to a normal human being that he allow himself to be turned into a low-browed caveman. The thought revolted him. And then I saw that this creature was no longer the Brilling I had known, but was a man of a million years from now, or more, a creature of a far-off, future time. And I realized that even more fully when I heard his plans, when I discovered what he had done in my absence.

"I found that instead of turning on the reversing ray after my departure, he had allowed the accelerating ray to stay on, and thus instead of bringing the plant-things back to harmless vegetation, he had allowed them to develop still further, to develop into active, intelligent creatures.

"He told me that, exultant, and when I could not believe, took me to the other end of the island. And there I saw the proof of his words, saw for the first time—the plant-men.

"I call them plant-men, for they were roughly human in shape, more human-shaped, in face, than Brilling himself. They walked erect on two limbs, and had two arms or feelers, and between their—shoulders—they carried a bulbous mass in which were set their eyes, two circles of blank, dead white, with which they could see. But there all human resemblance ceased, Owen. There were no other features in the blank faces, and the bodies, the mass of the things, seemed to be composed of dark-green fiber, coarse and stringy-looking. And, as Brilling told me, they remained true plants, for all their intelligence and activity, since they took in their food as inorganic materials, and utilized it by means of the chlorophyll in their bodies, a thing that only a true plant can do. Plants,

Owen, but moving, seeing, reasoning. The things knew Brilling, they were friendly to him, crowded around him, obeyed his orders. And he had allowed them to develop in hordes, and now boasted to me that they would be his servants, his agents, his armies.

"His armies! For that was the plan he revealed to me, that was his great scheme. He meant to develop great numbers of the things, to raise up a vast army of them on the island, then send them rushing out onto the world, having them make and take with them many powerful ray-projectors, which would be set up in the world outside, and which would sweep the earth with the accelerating ray. You see the result? They would spread the deadly accelerating ray over all the earth, and after all animal life had changed and passed, as it had done on the island, then the earth's plant-life would change, would evolve into new vast hordes of plant-men. They would go on, on, raising new hordes from the very ground itself, and finally, so Brilling said, when his hordes had swept over all the earth, they would reach out to other world, sweep from planet to planet in irresistible force.

*

"It was the plan of a crazed brain, Owen, a mad scheme that struck me through with horror. For I saw that Brilling could do it, could loose the hordes of the plant-men on the world, and sweep the earth with the accelerating ray. And I never doubted but that after he had done that, the plant-men would brush him from their path, after they had attained supremacy. But by then the evil would have been done. And Brilling was asking me to join him in his plan, was asking me to submit myself to the

accelerating ray and become a thing like himself, then join him in this terrible project.

"I knew better than to refuse him outright. I pretended to accept the suggestion, and we agreed to turn the accelerating ray on myself, the next day. And that night I fled from the island.

"I had planned to get into the laboratory and to the ray-projector, to turn on the reversing ray and reduce the hordes of plant-men to mere vegetation again. But when I crept down to the laboratory building late that night, I found it guarded by a score of the plant-men, and knew that Brilling was taking no chances. And I knew it would be impossible for me to break through that guard. I had a pistol, but who could kill a plant with a gun? And these plant-men were armed, armed with a strange weapon that threw intense, devouring flame, a daggerlike thing that spurted out puffs of flame and oxygen simultaneously, so that whatever received that flaming discharge took fire at once. Brilling had devised the weapon for them, and it was a terrible one, I knew.

"What could I do? If I stayed on the island I could do nothing, for the next day Brilling would turn on me the accelerating ray, making of me a monster like himself. And if I refused, he would kill me, I knew. So I made my way down to the beach, to the yawl there, and left the island, heading north for Cuba. I feared pursuit, for I knew the powers Brilling had at his command, but no pursuit came, and I got safety to Lluegos. And there I hesitated. What could I do? I could not spread the alarm and take a force down to the island to destroy the menace there. I knew that against Brilling's new weapons

such a force could do nothing. And who would have believed my story, had I told it? But if I could go back to the island, by stealth, if only with a single friend to help me, much might be done. So I caught a New York Steamer and came north, to you, the one person I thought I could count on.

"So I came. And now I must return. I came to ask you to go back with me. Even now we may be too late. But you know all now, Owen. Will you go back, with me?"

Owen's face expressed his doubt. "You know that I don't doubt your story, Walton, but it seems so utterly strange. It seems impossible that there could really be such a thing, such a menace—"

Walton spoke, solemnly. "There is such a menace, Owen. And it is a menace such as was never known before, a destroying blight that will blot out our world if it is not checked. Do you think I don't feel the strangeness of the thing? Coming north in the yawl, I felt myself going mad thinking of it. Down there on the island, Brilling, or the creature that once was Brilling, is working, planning, preparing, urging his hordes of plant-men on and on, coming nearer and nearer to the climax of his plans.

"And soon, out from the island will sweep the hordes of the plant-men, killing and spreading terror, setting up the ray-projectors and sweeping the world with the deadly accelerating ray. And then—horror and death and confusion undreamed of, over all earth. Familiar animals changing into hideous monsters, invasions of strange beasts, scourges of gigantic insects terrors, vast sea-things pulling down ships at sea, and, most horrible of all, men and women changing into shapes of

terror like Brilling, men and women changing into hideous creatures like him. A world of monstrous changes, a world where all life changes and passes, and then, at the last, a world where all animal life has died away and vanished forever. And then, the last great change, the plant-life of the world springing out into new and dreadful shapes, rising up into hordes of the plant- men. And at the end, reigning supreme from pole to pole—the plant-men." Walton ceased speaking, his face pale, his eyes burning. Owen rose from his chair, sickened by the picture the other had brought to his mind. Then, turning swiftly, he asked, "When do we leave, Walton?"

A faint smile passed over Walton's face, the first Owen had seen there since his return. "I knew I could count on you, Owen," he said. "There's a boat for Havana, Tuesday morning. We can get that."

*

Forty-eight hours later the two men stood at the rail of a fruit line steamer, watching the New York skyline fade into the distance behind them as the boat went down the bay. Neither spoke then.

Havana, then Lluegos, a colorful little port on the southern coast of Cuba. They wasted no time there, transferring their baggage at once to Walton's yawl, which had been held there for him. A few hours after reaching the port they were swinging out of the harbor in the yawl, a ketch-rigged craft with an auxiliary motor. Ahead, nearly three hundred miles of the Caribbean Sea lay between them and the island that was their destination.

Out of the harbor they went, past the spongers and fishing

boats, past a gleaming white pleasure-yacht, out to the blue open sea. Steadily the little boat forged south, under a dancing breeze. And braced against the mast, Owen looked out ahead, across the waters, wondering in his heart what soul-sickening horror they were rushing toward, what destroying terror lay in wait for them beyond the horizon. Night rushed swiftly down upon them, bringing with it the blazing tropic stars, and later the shining splendor of the full moon. Still Owen peered ahead, across the silvered moonlit waters, while at the wheel behind him, his face set and grim, Walton held south, south.

Once, that night, shortly before midnight, they passed a great liner that was heading north to Havana. It was a giant cruise-ship, its upper works ablaze with dazzling lights, its top deck crowded with swirling passengers, dancing to the music of the ship's orchestra. Across the waters the lilting melody came clearly to the two men, but they held to their course, unheeding.

A few at the rail of the big liner saw the speeding sailboat and idly speculated on its identity and errand. But none there dreamed the truth, none guessed the strangeness and greatness of the mission on which the yawl fled south, racing down toward the little island on which was centered the fate of all the world.

4

It was night when the yawl reached the island, a deep, thick night as yet unrelieved by the expected moon. For hours Owen and Walton had tensely scanned the sea ahead, and now, as they made out a distant, dark mass that stood out dimly against

the starlit sky, the tension of their nerves seemed to become even greater. In silence Owen stared at the place, while Walton expertly guided the little boat through a maze of rocks and shoals.

Silently they swept in toward the island, toward a long, sandy beach that gleamed in the faint starlight. A little channel indented the beach's outline, and into this Walton steered the yawl, its keel grating and grinding over the sand, then stopping entirely. Speaking in whispers, the two men secured the boat to a near-by boulder with cables, then discussed their plan of action.

At Walton's direction, Owen carefully adjusted the pad that protected his spinal nerve-centers from the deadly ray, Walton doing likewise. They then strove to come to a decision on their next step.

"The ray-projector is our best chance," Walton told the other. "If we can get to it, and turn on the reversing ray full power, it will wipe out all life on the island except ourselves. The island is long and narrow, with a high ridge at its center, running its full length, and the cottage and laboratory are on the southern end. I think that the main camp of the plant-men is on the eastern beaches, on the other side of the island from us. So we had best head toward the southern end at once, and try to make our way into the laboratory there."

Owen assented, and the two began to moved stealthily along the beach. After a short distance, Walton suddenly turned inland and started up the long slope toward the central ridge that was the back-bone of the island, Owen following in his steps. And as he followed, Owen noted the bareness of those

slopes, since they were only rock and sand. Not even the commonest forms of weeds or vegetation grew on them. Had every scrap of plant-life on the island been transformed by the accelerating ray, been changed into hordes of plant-men? He shuddered at the thought.

Half-way up to the ridge, Walton stopped abruptly and held up a warning hand. From somewhere in the darkness ahead came a thin, wailing sound, a high-pitched whispering that came and went and came again to their ears. As they listened it seemed to grow louder, nearer, and a few pebbles rattled down the slope from above. And now they could plainly hear the sound of feet, many feet, shuffling down the bare slope toward them.

Instantly the two had sprung to the concealing shadows of a nearby cluster of giant rocks, and lying crouched behind these, peered out at what might be approaching. They heard a louder sound of shuffling, tramping feet, then down the slope and into view came a mass of dark figures that moved steadily past their place of concealment, passing down the slope toward the beach. Not unlike a crowd of men, Owen thought, watching them pass in the dim mistiness of the starlight. As they filed by, their wailing whispers came clearly to his ears, the sibilant murmur of their speech.

Before half of the marching figures had gone by, a ghostly glow of white light had poured up from behind the ridge above, and now there floated up into the sky, like a shining bubble, the full moon, laving the scene before them with its molten silver light. As that revealing light poured down on the passing shapes, Owen grasped his companion's arm, with a sudden

agony of asking, lips repeating his croon-chant, he saw what had occurred.

The realization was like the sudden, blinding, and at the same time clarifying light that sometimes comes to epileptics just as they are going into a seizure. It was the thought that he had kept away on the horizon of his mind, the thought that now charged in on him with long leaps and bounds and then stopped and sat on its haunches and grinned at him while its long tongue lolled.

Of course, he should have known all these years what it was. He should have known that Mr. Eumenes was the worst thing in the world for him. He had known it, but, like a drug addict, he had refused to admit it. He had searched for the man. Yet he had known it would be fatal to find him. The rose-colored spectacles would swing gates that should never be fully open. And he should have guessed *what* and *who* Mr. Eumenes was when that encyclopedic fellow in the truck had singsonged those names.

How could he have been so stupid? Stupid? It was easy! He had *wanted* to be stupid! And how could the Mr. Eumenes-or-otherwise have used such obvious giveaway names? It was a measure of their contempt for the humans around them and of their own grim wit. Look at all the double entendres the salesman had given his father, and his father had never suspected. Even the head of the Bureau of Health and Sanity had been terrifyingly blasé about it.

Dr. Vespa. He had thrown his name like a gauntlet to humanity, and humanity had stared idiotically at it and never guessed its meaning. Vespa was a good Italian name. Jack didn't know what it meant, but he supposed that it had the same meaning as the Latin. He remembered it from his high school class.

As for his not encountering the salesman until now, he had been lucky. If he had run across him during his search, he would have been denied the glasses, as now. And the shock would have made him unable to cry out and betray the man. He would have done what he was so helplessly doing at this moment, and he would have been carted off to an institution.

How many other transies had seen that unforgettable face on the streets, the end of their search, and gone at once into that state that made them legal prey of the Bohas?

That was almost his last rational thought. He could no longer feel his flesh. A thin red curtain was falling between him and his senses. Everywhere it billowed out beneath him and eased his fall. Everywhere it swirled and softened the outlines of things that were streaking by—a large tree that he remembered seeing in his living room, a naked giant, his father, leaning against it and eating an apple, and a delicate little white creature cropping flowers.

Yet all this while he lived in two worlds. One was the passage downwards towards the Garden of Eden. The other was that hemisphere in which he had dwelt so reluctantly, the one he now perceived through the thickening red veil of his sight and other senses.

They were not yet gone. He could feel the hands of the black-clad officers lifting him up and laying him upon some hard substance that rocked and dumped. Every lurch and thud was only dimly felt. Then he was placed upon something softer and carried into what he vaguely sensed was the interior of one of the barracks.

Some time later—he didn't know or care when, for he had lost all conception or even definition of time—he looked up the deep everlengthening shaft of himself into the eyes of another Mr. Eumenes or Mr. Sphex or Dr. Vespa or whatever he called himself. He was in white and wore a stethoscope around his neck.

Beside him stood another of his own kind. This one wore lipstick and a nurse's cap. She carried a tray on which were several containers. One container held a large and sharp scalpel. The other held an egg. It was about twice the size of a hen's egg.

Jack saw all this just before the veil took on another shade of red and blurred completely his vision of the outside. But the final thickening did not keep him from seeing that Doctor Eumenes was staring down at him as if he were peering into a dusky burrow. And Jack could make out the eyes. They were large, much larger than they should have been at the speed with which Jack was receding. They were not the pale pink of an albino's. They were black from corner to corner and built of a dozen or so hexagons whose edges caught the light.

They twinkled.

Like jewels.

Or the eyes of an enormous and evolved wasp.